Matthew's Dream

April 23, 1992

Our dearest Matthew —

On your third birthday —

our sincere wishes that

<u>all</u> your dreams come true

love always
Mama

For Madeline and Luca

Matthew's Dream

Leo Lionni

Alfred A. Knopf 🐎 New York

A couple of mice lived in a dusty attic with their only child.
His name was Matthew. In one corner of the attic, draped with
cobwebs, were piles of newspapers, books, and
magazines, an old broken lamp, and the sad remains of a doll.
That was Matthew's corner.

The mice were very poor, but they had
high hopes for Matthew.
He would grow up to be a doctor, perhaps.
Then they would have Parmesan cheese
for breakfast, lunch, and dinner.
But when they asked Matthew what he
wanted to be, he said,
"I don't know. . . .
I want to see the world."

One day Matthew and his classmates
were taken to the museum.
It was the first time.

They were amazed at what they saw.
   There was a huge portrait
of King Mouse the Fourth, dressed like a general.
And next to it was a picture of cheese that made Matthew drool.
   There were winged mice that floated through the air
      and mice with horns and bushy tails.
   And mountains and rushing streams, and branches
bowing in the wind. The world is all here, thought Matthew.

Entranced, Matthew wandered from room to room
gazing at the paintings. There were some
that he didn't understand at first.
One looked like crusts of pastry, but when he
looked more carefully, a mouse emerged.

Then, turning a corner, Matthew found himself
face to face with another little mouse.
She smiled at him. "I am Nicoletta," she said.
"Aren't these paintings wonderful?"

That night Matthew had a strange dream.
He dreamed that he and Nicoletta
were walking, hand in hand, in an immense,
fantastic painting.

As they walked, playful patches of color shifted under their
feet, and all around them suns and moons moved gently
    to the sound of distant music.
Matthew had never been so happy. He embraced Nicoletta.
    "Let's stay here forever," he whispered.

Matthew woke with a start. He was alone.
Nicoletta had faded with his dream.
The gray dreariness of his attic corner appeared
to him in all its bleak misery.
Tears came to his eyes.

But then, as if by magic, what Matthew saw began to change.
The shapes hugged each other and the pale colors
of the messy junk heap brightened.
Even the crumpled newspapers now looked soft and smooth.
And from afar Matthew thought he heard the notes
of a familiar music.

He ran to his parents' corner.
"I know!" he said. "Now I know!
I want to be a painter!"

Matthew became a painter.
He worked hard and painted large canvases
filled with the shapes and colors of joy.

Then he married Nicoletta.
In time he became famous,
and mice from all over the world
came to see and buy his paintings.

His largest painting
now hangs in the museum.
When asked about the title,
Matthew smiles.
"The title?" he says
as if he had never thought
about it before.
"My dream."

Leo Lionni is internationally acclaimed as an artist, designer, sculptor, art director, and creator of books for children. He is the recipient of the 1984 American Institute of Graphic Arts Gold Medal and is a four-time Caldecott Honor Book winner for *Alexander and the Wind-Up Mouse*, *Frederick*, *Inch by Inch*, and *Swimmy*. His picture books, noted for being both playful and serious, are distinguished by their enduring moral themes, their graphic simplicity, and their brilliant use of collage.

THIS IS A BORZOI BOOK PUBLISHED BY ALFRED A. KNOPF, INC.

Copyright© 1991 by Leo Lionni
All rights reserved under International and Pan-American Copyright Conventions. Published in the United States by Alfred A. Knopf, Inc., New York, and simultaneously in Canada by Random House of Canada Limited, Toronto. Distributed by Random House, Inc., New York. Manufactured in the United States of America 10 9 8 7 6 5 4 3 2

Library of Congress Cataloging-in-Publication Data
Lionni, Leo, 1910-
Matthew's dream / by Leo Lionni.
p.   cm.
Summary: A visit to an art museum inspires a young mouse to become a painter.
ISBN 0-679-81075-7   ISBN 0-679-91075-1 (lib. bdg.) :
[1. Mice—Fiction. 2. Artist—Fiction. 3. Museums—Fiction.]
I. Title   PZ7.L6634Mat 1991 [E]—dc20   90-34242 CIP AC